Hip Hop Alien

the **Battle** of

Consciousness
and
Gangster Rap

Written by
Ivory Keyes

Hip Hop Alien

Contents

Introduction............................ 2
Chapter
1. The Source......................... 4
2. Shining Star....................... 9
3. Fantastic Voyage.................. 12
4. Reunited........................... 16
5. Start of the Ending................ 21
6. The Conspiracy.................... 26
7. The Cross........................... 31
8. Crime Wave....................... 34
9. Temperature's Rising............. 39
10. The Exodus....................... 41
11. Rebel Nation..................... 43
12. Life After Death................. 46

Hip Hop Alien

Introduction

Hip Hop Alien is a tale about two brothers of royal descent that are at war against each other. Separated at birth, the two brothers grew up in two entirely different worlds. Both brothers are born geniuses. One brother created conscious rap, and the other created gangster rap.

A covert war takes place on the planet of Mars. The two brothers use their music to influence the people on the planet. Hip Hop music and the planet are split into two warring factions. Only time will tell who will rule the universe and who will become a **Hip Hop Alien**.

<u>Hip Hop Alien</u>

Once upon a Time
On a planet far away
Beings of all kinds
Use to work hard and play
In the middle of the night
The stars were shining bright
One star fell from heaven
Like a radiant light
Star touched the whole land
With a microphone in hand
Illuminating a nation
With awareness of man…

Hip Hop Alien

Chapter 1
The Source

Queen Sheila moaned as tiny beads of sweat collected on her forehead. "Push my Queen!" said the Queen's midwife. Queen Sheila let out a sharp cry and a tiny head appeared, followed by a royal body. "It's a boy!" said the midwife. She handed the newborn Prince to the Queen. Queen Sheila gazed into her son's calming gray eyes and instantly fell in love.

As Queen Sheila cradled her newborn son, King Negus touched his son's right hand and knew that the child was agreeable. "He shall be called Binqi," said King Negus, a ruler of many." Queen Sheila smiled and said, "Our son shall be a blessing to man."

- later that night -

Queen Leslie and King Negus were relaxing in the King's quarters. As they laid in bed, King Negus placed his right hand upon the pregnant Queen's stomach and knew that the unborn child was disagreeable. "I see great perils and separation in our future," said King Negus. A tear rolled down

<u>Hip Hop Alien</u>

Queen Leslie's face. For she knew that the king would not tell a lie.

Queen Sheila was resting in her quarters and suddenly an overwhelming feeling of anxiety fell upon her. She grabbed her newborn son and rushed toward the exit. When Queen Sheila opened her front door, her bodyguard was nowhere in sight. Queen Sheila sprinted through the corridor and found her bodyguard lying dead in the middle of the floor.

Queen Sheila panicked. She continued to run through the corridor. Someone grabbed Queen Sheila and pulled her into a crevice. The Queen tried to scream but a large hand quickly covered her mouth. "It is I my Queen," whispered King Negus, "We are under attack."

King Negus led Queen Sheila and their newborn son to the shuttle port. "You have to get out of here," said King Negus. "Queen Leslie is conspiring to kill you and our newborn son. If you stay my Queen. I'm afraid she will succeed."

Queen Sheila begged the King to leave with her but there was not enough room for all of them to fit inside of the emergency space pod. King Negus placed his finger tips upon Queen Sheila's eyelids

Hip Hop Alien

and the Queen foresaw their son leading a large crowd of people.

King Negus kissed Queen Sheila and buckled her into the last emergency escape pod. "I will see you soon, my Queen," said King Negus. A tear rolled down Queen Sheila's face. King Negus placed his right hand upon his heart then held up his right hand with his palm facing outward. The door on the escape pod closed shut and the escape pod instantly ejected Queen Sheila into space.

As Queen Sheila gazed outside of the plate glass window, she saw the giant mothership explode into tiny little particles. Queen Sheila shouted, "Nooo!" She held her newborn son close to her bosom and cried.

- 1 hour later -

A ball of fire streaked across the midnight sky. Moments later, Queen Sheila's space pod crashed on the planet of Mars. The Queen slowly crawled from beneath the wreckage with her son nestled in her arms. Queen Sheila staggered through a grassy field, and stumbled onto a narrow road.

As the Injured Queen wandered along the winding road, a white pickup truck came barreling around a sharp corner. The passenger of the pickup

<u>Hip Hop Alien</u>

truck saw Queen Sheila walking in the middle of the street and yelled, "Stop!" The driver stomped on his brake pedal and the truck went into a skid, narrowly missing the Queen by mere inches.

Queen Sheila fainted. The young couple in the truck crept up on Queen Sheila. The young woman blurted out, "O my God. Is she dead?" The young man checked the Queen's vitals and Queen Sheila had a faint pulse. The couple placed Queen Sheila and her newborn son inside of their pickup truck and drove to the nearest hospital.

The young couple carried Queen Sheila and her newborn son into the hospital's emergency room. The young woman shouted, "Someone help us please. A Woman and child have been injured!" Nurses rushed Queen Sheila and her newborn son to the intensive care unit.

Queen Sheila lay helpless on a hospital bed. She grabbed a nurse's hand and the nurse felt a sudden jolt of energy. Queen Sheila fainted. The doctor performed CPR on Queen Sheila but he was unable to resuscitate her. "She's gone," said the doctor, "notify this woman's family and have them pick up her son." The nurse gazed at the doctor as if she was under a spell and said, "This woman has no family. I will adopt the child."

Hip Hop Alien

Prince Binqi was in the hospital's nursery room and Queen Sheila appeared with King Negus in spirit. They stood beside Prince Binqi's crib. Queen Sheila gently cradled the back of her son's neck and King Negus placed his right hand upon the young prince's heart. Suddenly, Prince Binqi began to levitate. The walls of the hospital slowly began to disappear. Surrounded by total darkness, Prince Binqi's body started transmitting light.

Hip Hop Alien

Chapter 2
Shining Star

- 9 Years Later -
- 10:45pm -

A light was shining beneath her son's bedroom door. Anna opened the door and found a Star composing music on his laptop computer. "It's getting late," said Anna, "and you got school in the morning." Star's eyes were glued to his computer screen.

Star asked his mother for just a little more time. "The Show is tomorrow," said Star. Anna told Star that he could stay up for 20 more minutes and after that, he had to go to bed.

- the talent show -

The sounds of idle chatter filled the auditorium. The overhead lights began to dim and the rambunctious crowd began to settle down. Anna and her husband patiently waited as the velvet curtain slowly slid open. A hip hop beat started to play and Star said this rhyme.

Hip Hop Alien

"I'm a star child
Here to
set the record straight
This is how it goes down
On a daily base
I'm an original
An I got a new flow
Niga my styles change up
Like a fashion show"

At the end of Star's performance the crowd was completely silent. They had never heard anything like hip hop music before. Anna and Lester started clapping and then a few other parents clapped. Needless to say, Star did not win the talent show.

- 5 years later -

Star entered through the front door of his parent's house and his parents were sitting on the living room sofa. Lester asked Star, "Have you decided what school you'd like to attend?"

Star mentioned a college that was more than 3 hours away and Anna became upset. Anna blurted out, "That's too far away!" She slammed her magazine on the sofa and rushed to her bedroom.

Hip Hop Alien

Lester went into the bedroom and sat on the bed with Anna.

Tears rolled down Anna's pretty face as she held Star's baby picture in her hand. Lester placed his arm around Anna's shoulders and Anna said, "Our little boy has grown up."

- 3 years later -

Star was at his college dormitory and his roommate asked, "Where will you be partying at for spring break?" Star told Carlos that he was going to go visit his parents. "Sucks to be you," said Carlos. Carlos tried to persuade Star to go on vacation with him but Star declined his invitation.

Lester and Anna were eating dinner at their kitchen table and Star entered through the front door. Star greeted his parents with warm hugs. He looked at Lester and said, "I have a present for you pop." Star pulled a media player out of his backpack and gave it to Lester. "It's over 2000 songs on there," said Star, "I even added my new album to your playlist." Lester thanked Star for the gift and then they embraced each other once more.

Hip Hop Alien

Chapter 3
Fantastic Voyage

Lester and three of his fellow astronauts climbed into the cockpit of a linear spacecraft. As Lester strapped himself into his seat, the commanding officer gave the signal for the countdown to began. The clock struck zero and the space shuttle's main engine propelled the giant spacecraft into the air.

Star stepped onto the stage of a local nightclub and the crowd went wild.

> "All I have is love
> All I want is peace
> All we got is us
> The truth is what I speak
> Open up your eyes negus
> Tell me what you see
> We are not the same
> But we are royalty"

Carlos and Angel were at the drink bar waiting for Star. As Star approached the bar area a strange man greeted him. Star shook the strange man's hand and knew that the man was agreeable. "With skills like that," said Alex, "I'm almost certain that I can get you a major recording deal." Alex gave Star a

Hip Hop Alien

business card and told Star to give him a call if he was interested.

- 10 months later -

Lester and his crew began to slowly descend onto the planet of Venus. The captain engaged the spacecraft's massive rocket thrusters and deployed the landing gear. A large steel ramp slowly extended to the Venusian surface. Lester hopped into the space buggy and his crew member Charlie, climbed into the passenger seat.

Twenty minutes into the expedition, Charlie spotted the opening to a cave. Lester parked the buggy and then he and Charlie crept into the cave. Huge rocks in the form of icicles hung from the cave's ceiling and pointy rocks pierced through the cave's floor. As Charlie and Lester ventured deeper into the cave, Lester's spectrometer spiked.

Lester noticed a hole in the cave's wall. Charlie and Lester squeezed through the narrow opening and a pointy rock punctured their space suits. The hole in the wall led to a large room that had strange markings scribed into the walls. As Lester and Charlie analyzed the Venusian manuscript, a yellow cloud permeated the room. The yellow mist seeped into Lester and Charlie's space suits and caused them to pass out.

Hip Hop Alien

Alex and Star were in a meeting with an executive from a major record label. Star played a few of his songs and the record executive leaned back in his black leather chair. "This sounds like a new genre of music," said the record executive. He offered Star $250,000 to sign a recording contract and Star accepted the offer.

Loud voices echoed through Charlie and Lester's two way radios. Lester and Charlie slowly began to regain consciousness. They opened their eyes and their pupils were glowing fluorescent yellow. "This is radio control," said Tim," do you read me?" Charlie replied, "We read you mission control, we're on our way."

As Star slept, he had a vision of being chased by a group of shadowy beings with fluorescent yellow eyes. Star ran as fast as he could but it was as if he was running in slow motion. He leaned forward and dug his fingers into the ground, scratching and pulling in an effort to elude his pursuers. Suddenly Star awoke drenched in sweat.

Hip Hop Alien

Lester and Charlie entered the main cabin. They opened their mouth's and a yellow cloud filled the cabin. Tom and Jayla inhaled the yellow mist and within seconds their eyes started glowing bright fluorescent yellow.

Star entered a convenience store near his college campus. After purchasing a few items, Star walked toward the exit and an older woman with long flowing white hair was standing near the doorway. "Young man," said the older woman. "Do you know who you are?" Star halted and then replied, "Who am I?"

The older woman's eyes started glowing fluorescent purple. "You are Prince Binqi, the first born son of King Negus," said the woman with the long flowing hair. "You must study yourself my prince, so that you may harness the power within."

Hip Hop Alien

Chapter 4
Reunited

- 7 months later -

Anna entered her home and saw Lester's luggage sitting on the foyer floor. She called Lester's name but he did not answer. Anna went to her bedroom and found Lester laying in a bathtub full of ice. "Are you okay?" asked Anna as she watched Lester sweat profusely.

Late one night, a huge spacecraft landed in a remote area of Mars. A steel ramp slowly extended onto the Martian surface and a tall man with dark skin exited the giant spacecraft. After taking a few steps, the man and his spaceship vanished into thin air.

Star and Carlos were awakened by a loud knock on their bedroom door. Carlos opened the door as he wiped the cold from his eyes and said, "Who do you want?" King Negus placed his right hand on Carlos's shoulder and Carlos passed out.

Star arose from his bed and started communicating with King Negus through mental telepathy. "My father," said Star. "I am," replied

Hip Hop Alien

King Negus. "Your brother has found your location. You must learn to out think him."

Anna and Lester were at the General Hospital. "Try not to move," said the MRI technician. The table slowly slid into a large tube as Lester tried his best to stay still. The radiologist stood speechless with his mouth gaped wide open. Anna asked the radiologist if everything was ok and he replied, "I've never seen anything like this before."

Star entered the convenience store near his college campus. He asked the cashier if she knew where the old woman with the long white hair was. The cashier had no idea who Star was talking about.

Star gave the cashier a detailed description of the older woman. He even described the cashier that was working on the day that the woman with the long white hair was at the store. The cashier did not recall anyone matching the descriptions that Star had given to her ever working or being at the store.

<u>Hip Hop Alien</u>

- later that night -

As Star stood backstage he seemed to be aloof. Alex asked Star if everything was alright and Star said he was good. The host gave Star a formal introduction and then Star walked onto the stage. The crowd went wild and Star began to rhyme.

"You now rockin whit
the all mighty lyrical
The O-riginal man
I'm something like a miracle"

As Star performed, he spotted a man standing in the crowd with bright fluorescent yellow eyes. Although Star had never seen the man before, he somehow felt that the two of them were connected to each other.

Shaquille stepped off of an elevator accompanied by two large men bearing a pair of fluorescent yellow eyes. They entered the CEO's office and demanded the CEO to sign his record label over to Shaquille. "And why would I do that?" said the CEO. The two muscle bound men grabbed the CEO by his ankles and dangled him out of the 33rd story window. The CEO shouted, "Okay! I will sign it!"

<u>Hip Hop Alien</u>

A stretch limousine pulled up to a luxurious 5 star hotel. Alex hopped out of the limousine, followed by Star and Angel. As they checked into their hotel rooms, the bellhop gathered everyone's luggage.

Star and Angel entered their hotel suite. Angel took a hot shower and Star sat down on the king size bed. The bellhop knocked on the door and Star told him to come in. He placed their luggage inside of the closet and left.

Moments later, Angel walked out of the bathroom with a towel wrapped around her petite frame. Angel asked Star if the bellhop brought their bags up. Star pointed at the closet and Angel opened the sliding closet door. She unzipped her duffel bag and let out an intense scream.

Angel slammed the closet door and jumped onto the bed with Star. She crouched down behind Star and whispered, "There's a little green man in my bag." Star gazed at Angel in disbelief. He opened the closet door and there was a little green man standing inside of Angel's duffle bag.

Hip Hop Alien

Star grabbed the small being by his neck and lifted him into the air. The little green man flailed its arms and legs. "What the hell are you?" shouted Star. "My name is Rap," the little man replied, "I am your humble servant."

Star placed his right hand upon Rap's heart and knew that Rap was agreeable. "I have grave news for you master," said Rap. "Your brother is conspiring to destroy you. If he succeeds, the quality of life for your people on this planet will decline drastically."

Hip Hop Alien

Chapter 5
Start of the Ending

As Shaquille sat behind his desk, he called his secretary and told her to send in the next artist. The office door crept open and a timid teenager entered Shaquille's office. The teenager connected his cell phone to a USB cord and played a few of his songs for Shaquille.

After playing a few songs the timid teenager asked Shaquille if he liked his music. Shaquille opened his mouth and a yellow cloud filled the room. The teenager inhaled the yellow mist and became hypnotized. His eyes started glowing bright fluorescent yellow. "Your name Shall be Young Murder," said Shaquille.

Star stepped onto the stage of a local nightclub and the crowd roared with excitement. The DJ dropped a beat and Star started rhyming.

<u>Hip Hop Alien</u>

"In the image of God
I'm a born King
I got knowledge of self
Now watch me do my thing
I tell you what it is
An that's just what it be
No one can keep
a niga down
it's like
I have wings"

- after Star's performance -

Angel, Alex and Star were on their way back to their hotel and Star heard his name being mentioned on the radio. Star asked Alex, "Did he just say my name?" Alex turned the volume up on the radio and everyone listened closely.

"Star be talkin bout peace
Ain't no muhfuckin peace
Ain't no got dam Love
For these negus
an these freaks
I put the hammer
to dat bamma
Press his cheek whit the heat
Beat him in his fuckin head
Take his bread

<u>Hip Hop Alien</u>

> now he can't eat
> Cuz I'm the shit
> I'm the shit
> I'm da mothafukin shit...
> I be breakin Bad!
> My niga cuz I'm the shit"

The DJ shouted, "That's the new hit from Young Murder!" The sound of artificial bombs exploded over the track as the DJ repeatedly played Young Murder's song.

Anna entered her home and found Lester floating face down in the swimming pool. She managed to pull Lester's naked body out of the swimming pool and administer CPR, but Lester was non respondent. Anna quickly dialed 911 and told the operator to send an ambulance immediately.

- 1 week later -

As the pastor delivered Lester's eulogy, Anna dried her tears with a white handkerchief. Star placed his arm around Anna's shoulders and escorted her to a black limousine. "If it's not too much to ask right now," said Star, "I would like to move back home." Anna's face lit up and she replied, "I would love that."

Hip Hop Alien

A yellow mist filled the recording booth as Young Murder laid his rhyme.

"I got money on my mind
so I'm chasing it
Pumpin blow
an blowin money
Yeah that's basic shit
Big boys they don't cry
They just take the risk
Either I'll make it
Or I'll take it
It is what it is"

As patrons partied at a local nightclub, Shaquille ordered a bottle of champagne and patiently watched the crowd from his VIP section. The DJ played one of Young Murder's song's and the crowd became enraged. Suddenly a huge fight broke out on the dance floor.

Shaquille sipped from his champagne bottle and smiled. A beautiful waitress sashayed through a mob of angry partiers and made her way to Shaquille. The waitress reached Shaquille unscathed. She asked Shaquille if he was enjoying the show.

Hip Hop Alien

The waitress gave Shaquille a card that had the imprint of a bird on it and said, "call me." Shaquille looked into the waitresses eyes and said, "I can see through your disguise." The waitress winked at Shaquille and revealed her vertical slit pupils. "I know you can," replied the waitress. She walked away and dragged her reptilian tail on the floor behind her.

Hip Hop Alien

Chapter 6
The Conspiracy

A group of teenagers were hanging out at a neighborhood play park. Star's album was blasting through a Bluetooth speaker. A teenager blurted out, "Star is some trash. Young Murder dat niga!" The teenager synced his cell phone up to the Bluetooth speaker and told everyone to listen closely.

> "It's us against them my niga
> Time to squad up
> Gangbang my niga
> Tear your squad up
> Bullets hit up yo whip
> Tear yo car up
> I'm gonna get you niga
> Leave you scarred up"

Shaquille met with the waitress from the nightclub at a secret location. There were over two dozen wealthy businessmen and women in attendance. The waitress stood in front of a huge round table and made an announcement. She said, "We all are gathered here tonight because we share a common enemy."

<u>Hip Hop Alien</u>

The waitress told the group that she had a plan that would get rid of their enemies. "Tonight I proudly present to you our newest venture," said the waitress. "Private prisons." The waitress told Shaquille that she would promote his music all over the world as long as his artists encouraged the masses to use drugs and commit acts of violence.

- 9 months later -

Anna, Star and Angel were watching the evening news and a reporter asked the question, "Is hip hop music the reason for the sudden increase in crime?" The camera panned to Shaquille and Shaquille stared into the camera's lens and replied, "those allegations are false and totally baseless."

Star gazed at the television and blurted out loud, "why does this guy look so familiar?" Rap responded, "That's your half brother, Prince Shaquille." Anna saw Rap and passed out. "Damn it Rap!" Star shouted, "You weren't supposed to let her see you!"

- a few minutes later -

Anna slowly regained consciousness. She asked Star, "What in the world is that?" Anna pointed at Rap and Rap exhaled a purple cloud. Anna inhaled the purple haze and instantly became enlightened.

Hip Hop Alien

Teenagers rushed into the amphitheater by the thousands to see Young Murder and his label mates perform. The female rap duo, Kitty & Kat, opened the concert with their sexualized lyrics. The world famous womanizer, Mr. Mac and the infamous rap group DDS (Drug Dealer Surplus) went on stage afterwards. Young Murder was the last act to step onto the stage.

The audience chanted, "Murder! Murder! Murder!" Young Murder gazed upon the audience and a sea of bright fluorescent yellow eyes were staring back at him. The DJ dropped a beat and Young Murder said this rhyme.

"It's Young Murder bitch!
I'm Dam near insane
I put your lights out
Just for sayin my name
Now say my name
say my name
Like it's destiny
An I'm ah come through
With the gang
packin heavy heat"

Two teenage boys were having a debate in front of a neighborhood convenience store. One teenager told the other that Young Murder was the greatest

Hip Hop Alien

rapper of all times. A sedan with dark tinted windows crept up beside the two teenagers. The windows quickly rolled down and multiple shots were fired at the two teens. They fell to the ground and the sedan drove off into the night.

Star and Alex were sitting at Anna's kitchen table. Alex told Star that the radio stations haven't been playing his music lately. "We need to get you in the studio ASAP" said Alex.

- later that night -

Star stepped into the recording booth and started rhyming.

"Radio won't play my songs
Cause I speak the truth
Other rappers
They be scams
Tryna make the news
Tellin you to catch a body
But who catchin you?
Crooked police
Pull you over
Just to question you"

Anna and Rap were watching television. Rap looked over at Anna and said, "I sense anxiety within you. Would you like to talk about it?" Anna

Hip Hop Alien

sighed. Her eyes overflowed with tears. "My husband is dead," said Anna. "And on top of that, my son is an alien."

Rap placed his fingers upon Anna's eyelids and Anna began to see the future. Anna saw a world that was filled with war. She then saw Star raising multitudes of people up from the dead.

Shaquille was meditating and he had a vision of Queen Leslie floating amidst a yellow cloud. Queen Leslie and prince Shaquille conversed through mental telepathy. "Mother," said Shaquille. "I have found my brother. He is weak. I will destroy him and become the ruler of the universe."

Queen Leslie's pupils started glowing fluorescent yellow. "Do not underestimate your brother," said Queen Leslie. "For he does not yet know his full potential. If he ever gains knowledge of self, weak he will no longer be."

Hip Hop Alien

Chapter 7
The Cross

Star was walking through the local shopping mall with Rap hidden inside of his backpack. "Master," said Rap, "I sense someone is following us." Star ducked into the restroom and locked himself inside of a toilet stall. Someone entered the restroom and within seconds they were gone.

Star stepped out of the toilet stall and a large man Instantly appeared. The large man approached Star with one hand tucked inside of his coat pocket. He yanked his hand out of his pocket and revealed a cell phone. "Will you take a picture with me?" asked the large man. Star took a picture with the man and continued to walk through the shopping mall.

Suddenly Star heard a loud roar reverberate throughout the hallway of the shopping mall. Rap poked his head out of Star's backpack and saw a hairy 9ft monster running towards them. Frantic Pedestrians screamed and ran in all directions. Rap shouted, "Master! Watch your back!"

Rap hopped out of Star's backpack and landed on top of the hairy monster's shoulders. He wrapped his tiny legs around the monster's huge neck and placed his hands over the monster's temples. The

Hip Hop Alien

monster's fluorescent yellow eyes turned purple and Rap began to control the monster's mind.

Star saw another giant monster at the far end of the hall. The giant monster ran towards Star, smashing windows and destroying display cases along the way. "Rap!" shouted Star, "here comes another one!"

Star spotted a little girl hiding beneath a wooden bench. He ran incredibly fast but to him everything looked as if he was moving in slow motion. Star picked the little girl up and brought her to safety. When Star returned to the hallway the two gigantic monsters were fighting each other.

Star held his hands out with his palms facing upward. He began to meditate. A purple wave of light rippled from Star's body and transmitted throughout the shopping mall. Suddenly everyone calmed down and the giant monsters became docile.

Anna and Angel's favorite television show was abruptly interrupted by breaking news. A clip was shown of Star and two hairy monsters destroying the shopping mall. Anna and Angel looked at each other in disbelief. Moments later Star came barreling through the front door.

Hip Hop Alien

Anna asked Star if he was okay. "What have you done?" said Anna. "The police are looking for you." Star assured Anna that he did not hurt anyone. He then hurried to his bedroom and closed the door.

Rap climbed out of Star's backpack. "What happened back there?" said Star, "It felt like everything was moving in slow motion." Star's eyes were glowing bright fluorescent purple. "You are becoming aware of yourself," replied Rap.

- 11pm -

Star was awoken by the sound of Anna protesting loudly in the living room. Moments later Star's bedroom door flew open and two police officers rushed in with their guns drawn. Rap looked on from Star's closet as the police officers arrested Star.

Hip Hop Alien

Chapter 8
Crime Wave

Shaquille leaned back in his black leather chair and puffed on a freshly lit cigar. As Shaquille exhaled the sweet cigar smoke, Star's capture and arrest was being broadcast on the evening news. Shaquille displayed a sinister grin and his eyes started glowing bright fluorescent yellow.

Star patiently waited behind the plate glass window as Anna and Angel sat down on the other side. Angel unzipped her tote bag and Rap poked his head out. "This is the work of Prince Shaquille," said Rap. "You must ready yourself, for the battle is near."

4 gang members stuffed hollow tipped rounds into extended magazines. One gang member shoved an extended clip into a 9 millimeter Glock. He cocked his pistol and said, "It's time for some payback!"

Young Murder was at a radio interview and the question was asked, "So how does it feel to be the number one selling rap artist in the history of rap music?" Young Murder smiled and replied, "It's nothing, everyone knows I murder the competition."

Hip Hop Alien

    4 gang members crept down a long gravel filled driveway. At the end of the driveway was a little white house and a sedan that matched the description of the sedan that witnesses claimed to have seen during the shooting at the neighborhood convenience store.

    One gang member peeked inside the window of the little white house and another gang member kicked the front door open. The gang members rushed inside of the house with their guns drawn. They emptied their entire clips into 3 young men that were sitting in the living room and then they quickly vanished into the night.

    As Star slept on his jail bunk, he had a vision of Queen Sheila floating amidst a purple cloud. "Mother," said Star. "I have failed." Queen Sheila replied, "You mustn't give up. Use your time wisely and focus your mind."

    Star woke up and heard a group of inmates talking about him. He glanced at the inmates and then quickly looked away. One inmate said to another, "He just woke up. You should go holla at him."

<u>Hip Hop Alien</u>

    An inmate approached Star and asked Star to say a rhyme. Star was reluctant, but then he said this rhyme.

>"Lockdown
>In the belly
>of a smelly beast
>Where da police
>Try an tell me
>how to live and eat
>I'm a prince
>I'm a star
>I'm a born King
>An if I fall
>I come back
>like a boomerang
>I'm not a sucker
>cuz I rap about unity
>Cuz in the end all we really
>got is You and me"

The inmates applauded and the energy in the cell block was good.

    As Jalisa twerked and twirled her petite body around a gold stripper pole, Kitty & Kat's, "Good Pussy Song" blared through a pair of 30 inch woofers. After a long night of dancing, Jalisa made

Hip Hop Alien

her way to her car. She opened her trunk and placed her suitcase inside. Suddenly the blade of a cold steel knife was pressed against Jalisa's neck.

A large man wearing leather gloves and a baseball cap covered Jalisa's mouth. "Scream and I'll cut you!" said the large man. He pulled Jalisa's mini skirt up to her waist and sexually assaulted her in the parking lot.

A heroin addict entered the back door of an abandoned building. He approached two teenagers as they listened to the rap group DDS on their players. The addict purchased two capsules of heroin mixed with fentanyl and then went into an empty room. He injected himself with the fentanyl mix and overdosed with a syringe still stuck in his arm.

- 3 months later -

Jalisa patiently waited in the lobby of a health clinic. A nurse called Jalisa's name and escorted her to an examination room. After a short conversation, a doctor performed an abortion on Jalisa. Weak and heavily sedated, she caught a taxi to her apartment.

Jalisa passed out in the back seat of the taxicab. The driver wrapped his arm around her waist and escorted her to her apartment. He placed Jalisa's

Hip Hop Alien

relaxed body on her living room sofa. Seeing that she was unconscious, the taxi driver pulled Jalisa's panties down and had unprotected sex with her.

As Shaquille sat at the round table with his allies, the waitress from the nightclub stood up and congratulated everyone on their most recent and successful venture. "We have managed to enslave our enemies and get paid for it," said the waitress from the nightclub. "All of this would not have been made possible if it weren't for the help of our newest ally and friend, Prince Shaquille." Everyone stood to their feet and applauded.

Shaquille stood up and said, "When I joined this group, I assumed we all wanted the same thing." Faint mumbling and whispers filled the room. "Quiet!" shouted the waitress from the nightclub. "So what do you have in mind?"

Hip Hop Alien

Chapter 9
Temperature's Rising

Dark clouds blackened the early morning sky and a torrential rain was released upon the land and sea. Suddenly a hideous monster arose from the ocean and walked onto the shore. After taking a few steps, the monster spotted the photo of a handsome young man on a billboard. The monster morphed into the young man's image and continued to walk through the pouring rain.

Jalisa's cell phone rang and she woke up laying on her sofa with her panties down to her ankles. She answered her cellular phone and the doctor said, "I have something very important to tell you. I'm sad to say this but you are HIV positive."

Star had a vision of Rap floating amidst a purple cloud. "Master," said Rap. "Prince Shaquille is planning another attack." Star then had another vision of people starving and fighting each other in the streets. Suddenly Star woke up drenched in sweat.

Hip Hop Alien

An elite group of scientists conducted a secret clinical trial. As the scientist looked on from a secure location, 2 volunteers stood in a 10 by 10ft, plate glass examination room. A yellow mist filled the examination room and within seconds the volunteers began to sweat profusely. Their pupils started glowing bright fluorescent yellow and they became very aggressive. One volunteer struck the other and then the volunteers fought each other to the death. The surviving volunteer started eating the dead volunteer's flesh.

A police officer spotted a man walking downtown with a hoodie on. The man glanced at the police officer and then took off running. He ran into a nearby alleyway and the police officer chased the man into a dead end. "Put your hands up!" shouted the police officer.

The man raised his hands in the air and the police officer approached the man from behind. Slowly the man turned around. The man's face was scaly and his pupils were slit vertically. The police officer urinated on himself and started trembling.

The lizard man grabbed the police officer's neck and hoisted him into the air. He placed the palm of his hand on the police officer's head and then ripped the officer's face off.

Hip Hop Alien

Chapter 10
Exodus

Star was watching the evening news and the anchor said, "An unknown virus is infecting people and making them incredibly violent." The camera panned to a gruesome scene. Crowds of people were on the streets, fighting and killing each other. "This is pure Pandemonium!" said the news anchor.

An inmate fell to the floor and started having convulsions. One inmate ran to the bars and shouted, "We need a nurse in here! Someone's having a seizure!" Two nurses rushed into the cell block followed by three correctional officers. Suddenly a group of inmates overpowered the correctional officers and forced their way out of the cell block.

Angel and Rap were watching television and their regularly scheduled program was interrupted by breaking news. "144 inmates have just escaped from the city jail," said the Anchorman. Anna's doorbell rang. Rap and Angel looked at each other almost simultaneously. Angel opened the front door and Star was standing on the porch.

Hip Hop Alien

A 16-year-old boy was walking home one night from a neighborhood convenience store. The boy was anemic. And on top of all that, it was a cold and rainy night.

As the young boy walked beneath the dimly lit street lights, he had a black hoodie on and his hands were tucked inside of his pockets. A police car slowly crept up from behind the teen and abruptly stopped beside him. Two police officers jumped out of the patrol car and started harassing the teenager.

The police officers wrestled the young teen to the ground. One of the officers placed his knee on the back of the teenager's neck. The teenager shouted, "I can't breathe!" And with his last breath, the teen called for his mother. One police officer said to the other, "I think he's dead."

Shaquille was at his office, talking to the man with the scaly face. "A war is about to take place," said Shaquille. "What side of history will you be on?" The man leaned back in his chair. His pupils started glowing fluorescent yellow. Gilla replied, "I think we both know the answer to that question."

Hip Hop Alien

Chapter 11
Rebel Nation

Star was at a recording studio with two of the escaped inmates. As Star sat behind the mixing board, the two inmates stepped into the recording booth and said this rhyme.

Inmate #1:
"I was down bad
Kidnapped like a slave
Inmate #2:
Treated like a animal
They threw me in a cage
Inmate #1:
I woke up
Half sleep
In a shallow grave
Inmate #2:
An now I'm tryna
wake my people up
From a daze"

Homicide detectives were investigating the murder of a slain police officer found decapitated in an alleyway. As blood and skin tissue lay scattered throughout the alleyway, one detective said to another, "This looks like the work of a monster."

Hip Hop Alien

The detective looked his colleague in the eye and replied, "This is the work of a monster."

Protesters gathered in front of the City Hall in protest of a 16 year old boy that was murdered by two on duty police officers. The protesters chanted, "No justice! No peace! No hating ass police!" The police tried to break the crowd up but that only made matters worse. The protesters started setting cars and buildings on fire.

Protesters continued to burn, loot, and riot throughout the city. For eight consecutive weeks the streets reeked of anarchy. A huge civil war took place. The planet became divided between the followers of Shaquille, the authoritarian oppressor, and the non-conforming followers of Star.

- 4 months later -

Shaquille forced his followers to take oaths and insert computer chips into their bodies. He then placed soldiers in front of every grocery store and hospital on the planet. Only those who pledged total allegiance to Shaquille were allowed access to food and medical treatment.

Star led his family and his followers far away from the inner city. They settled upon a plot of land hidden deep in the wilderness. With the help of his

Hip Hop Alien

followers, Star built homes for his people to live in, and he also created medicine from the plants and herbs that grew on the land.

Star stood before his followers and made an announcement. "This is our land," said Star. "My only request is that no one indulge in the opium plant." Everyone agreed to Star's request and all was well.

One day a young man took the immature seeds of the opium plant and ground them into a fine powder. He then inhaled the opium powder and fell asleep. The young man's wife came home and noticed her husband had become dull and inactive. The wife asked her husband, "What's the matter with you?" The young man told his wife what he had done. He then persuaded his wife to partake of the opium powder.

As Shaquille sat at the round table with his allies, everyone was celebrating except for him. Gilla noticed the angry expression fixed upon Shaquille's face. He leaned toward Shaquille and said, "you don't seem too happy." Shaquille looked into Gilla's vertically slit pupils and said, "This war is not over until my brother is dead!"

Hip Hop Alien

Chapter 12
Life After Death

As Rap meditated a seraphim appeared amidst a purple cloud. "You must leave this planet," said the seraphim. Rap asked the seraphim if the planet was going to be destroyed and the seraphim replied, "Yes. The inhabitants of this planet have become wicked, they are stubborn and unchangeable."

Filled with grief, Rap asked the seraphim, "Will those that are agreeable also be killed?" The seraphim sympathized with Rap and said, "If there are any humans that are agreeable, they will be spared."

The seraphim arrived at Star's village in the evening and Star was sitting near the front gate. When Star saw the seraphim, he stood up and greeted her. Star introduced himself to the seraphim and said, "Come with me to my house. You can get some rest and continue on your travels in the morning." The seraphim replied, "No thanks, I will find my own place to rest." Star was persistent. He insisted that the seraphim go with him and eventually she agreed.

Hip Hop Alien

The seraphim went with Star and entered his house. Angel and Anna prepared a meal for the seraphim and they ate. Star heard a knock at his front door. He answered the door and all of the men in the village were standing in front of his house. One man asked Star, "Where is the woman that I saw you with tonight? Send her out so we can have our way with her."

Star stepped outside and closed the door behind him. "I brought her to my house so that she will be safe," said Star. "I will not let you harm her." The crowd became angry and a man shouted, "Go get her or we will go in and get her ourselves!"

A man approached Star and the seraphim reached out and pulled Star back into the house. Star looked at the seraphim and her eyes started glowing bright fluorescent purple. The seraphim told Star to get his family out of the village. Star quickly gathered his family.

The seraphim stepped outside and struck her hands together. A bright light rippled throughout the village and blinded the men that were standing in front of Star's house. The seraphim told Star and his family to run and never look back. As Star and his family were running, Anna looked back and instantly burst into flames.

Hip Hop Alien

A purple beam of light shot down from the night sky. The seraphim appeared inside the beam of light. Star, Angel and Rap ran into the light and were instantly transported into a giant spacecraft.

The spacecraft hovered above the surface of Mars. Suddenly a white beam of light shot from beneath the giant spacecraft and scorched the planet's surface. Within seconds all life on the planet was destroyed.

The huge black spacecraft dashed into the sky. Moments later the giant spacecraft hovered above the planet of Tiamat. The seraphim said to Star, "Everything on this planet shall be under your dominion." A tear rolled down Rap's face. Star asked Rap why he was crying and Rap replied, "I will not be coming with you master."

Rap placed his right hand upon his heart and then held up his right hand with his palm facing outward and then Star and Angel did the same. Within seconds, Star and Angel were beamed onto the surface of Tiamat. Star and Angel looked up in the sky and the huge black spacecraft quickly disappeared into thin air.

- To be continued -

Hip Hop Alien

Printed in Great Britain
by Amazon